McGinty'

Written by Diana Noonan
Illustrated by June Joubert

Melissa Brown loved cats.

She loved the black cat at the corner store.

She loved the gray cat at the dairy.

She loved the tabby cat at the video store. He rubbed his back against Melissa's legs, and he looked at her with green eyes.

But best of all, Melissa loved McGinty.

She patted his coat. "You're so soft," she said. "You're so gentle and warm."

Melissa wanted a cat of
her own, but the Browns
had canaries. "Please! Please!"
said Melissa. "Pl-e-a-s-e may
I have just a tiny kitten?"

"I'm sorry," said Mr. Brown.
"Kittens grow into cats, and
the canaries were here first.
Cats and canaries do not mix,
Melissa."

Melissa hissed, "I'm not Melissa!
I'm Marmalade, the cat!
I'm McGinty's friend!"

When Melissa went to bed,
she curled up like a cat on
a pillow.

Mr. Brown came in with her
cocoa. She hissed at him again
and showed her claws. "I'm
going to lap my cocoa from the
saucer," she growled. "And leave
my light off! I can see in the
dark."

Mr. Brown laughed. He went
to cover the canary cages.

When everyone was sleeping, Melissa jumped through her window. She landed in the yard on velvet paws.

"McGinty," she meowed quietly. "McGinty."

McGinty came to the gate. "I'm going to the park," he said. "Come on!"

At the park, McGinty met his friends. Melissa had never seen so many cats. They sat on the seesaw and perched on the swings. They sat on the picnic tables. They scratched their claws on the park benches.

But Melissa had no time to talk to them. McGinty had shot up like a furry rocket, into a tree.

McGinty's friends went up the tree, too. "Coming?" they called to Melissa.

"Are you a scaredy cat?" asked McGinty.

"Of course not," said Melissa. She climbed up to the first branch. But when she got to the second branch, a fat tabby cat cried, "To the wall!"

All around her, the cats

their way down the trunk, and

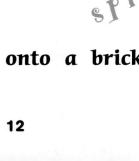

onto a brick wall.

Melissa pulled herself up the wall. She teetered like a tightrope walker after the cats.

At the end of the wall, McGinty jumped onto the roof of the corner store. "Come on!" he said.

Melissa was terrified. "You just have to jump," said a pretty little cat. "It's not hard."

"But I thought cats were quiet creatures," cried Melissa.

"We are quiet in the day time," said McGinty, "but at night, we play."

"I don't like your games," said Melissa. "You'll have to play without me."

15

In the morning, Melissa woke up in her own bed. When she went to get her breakfast, Mr. Brown said, "Your breakfast is on the floor, Marmalade. I hope you like sardines and milk."

"I'm not Marmalade," said Melissa. "I'm Melissa. Don't call me Marmalade anymore. I don't want a cat now. Cats are very nice . . . but I would rather play with canaries!"

Narratives

What's a narrative?

A narrative is a story that has a plot (or storyline) with:

An introduction

A problem

A solution

How to Write a Narrative

Step One Write an introduction
An introduction tells the reader:

- Who the story is about (the characters)
- Where the story takes place (the setting)
- When the story happened

Step Two **Write about the problem**
Tell the reader about:

- The events of the story and the problems that the main characters face
- What the characters <u>do</u> about the problem

> Keeping up with McGinty is really hard!

Step Three **Write about the solution**
Tell the reader how the problem is solved.

Don't forget!
A narrative can have more than one main character.

We are the main characters.

We are the other characters.

19

▬▬ **Guide Notes**

Title: McGinty's Friend
Stage: Fluency (1)

Text Form: Narrative
Approach: Guided Reading
Processes: Thinking Critically, Exploring Language, Processing Information
Written and Visual Focus: Illustrative Text

THINKING CRITICALLY
(sample questions)
- How do you know that this story is fiction?
- Why do you think Mr. Brown said cats and canaries don't mix?
- How do you know Melissa didn't like to be called a scaredy cat?
- What do you think really made Melissa change her mind about cats?
- Why do you think Melissa thought cats were quiet creatures?

EXPLORING LANGUAGE

Terminology
Spread, author and illustrator credits, ISBN number

Vocabulary
Clarify: hissed, canaries, velvet, perched, tabby, teetered, tightrope
Nouns: cat, store, coat, canaries, pillow
Verbs: hiss, growl, jump, meow, perch, claw
Singular/plural: leg/legs, cat/cats, bed/beds, table/tables
Simile: shot up like a furry rocket, teetered like a tightrope walker

Print Conventions
Apostrophes – possessives (Melissa's legs, McGinty's friend), contraction (I'm, you're)

Phonological Patterns
Focus on short and long vowel **a** (cats, lap, patted, Marmalade, games)
Discuss root words – rubbed, patted, hissed, canaries, terrified, coming
Look at suffix **ly** (quietly)
Discuss the silent letter in – **w**rote